JD SNYDER

REDEMPTION

COURAGE   FAITH

God Bless!

JD

THE
TALE OF TWO
THIEVES
THE UNTOLD STORY

The Tale of Two Thieves
Copyright © 2013 by Joseph Snyder. All rights reserved.

First Print Edition: February 2013

Nomadic Heretic Inc.

Published by Nomadic Heretic, Inc.
4888 N Kings Hwy #217
Fort Pierce, FL 34951

Printed in the United States of America

ISBN: 978-1-62480-065-8 (Print)

DEDICATION

It is late November, 2012, as I pen the last few words to this story. It will soon be five years since my life ended...life as I knew it. I accepted Christ as my Lord and Savior in 1978, when I was just 19 years old... while serving in the US Navy. When our ship stopped over in Israel, I traveled to Jerusalem where I was able to see the story of Jesus' crucifixion unfold before my very eyes. I will never forget the time that I spent there or the impact that it made on me.

On December 5th, 2007, my son, Captain Adam P. Snyder, US Army (who was a West Point graduate and Airborne Ranger) was killed in action with two of his men in Iraq.

The death of my only child caused me not only to lose my will to live... but also my faith in God.

Today, I am writing this dedication as a new man, for God has not only restored my will to live, but also my passion and zest for life. He has instilled in me more joy and hope than I have ever possessed ... and my love for humanity knows no bounds.

But these things pale compared to the one gift my Lord has bestowed upon me ... the gift of inner peace and serenity.

I have an inner peace and an understanding that I did not believe was possible. How I so much wish to share my gift with you, but I do not possess the power to do so. It is a gift from God and only he can bestow it upon you. The only thing that I can offer you is this simple story that holds the *keys* to understanding what truths he has enlightened me with, so you may also find your path to the same gift that he has given me....Inner Peace and Serenity.

I have shared a little of my life with you, so when I dedicate this book to my Lord and Savior Jesus Christ, you will understand my sincerity in using these words.

The book is dedicated to my Lord and Savior ... The story is for you.

JD Snyder

CHAPTER ONE

THE LIGHT OF THE NEW DAWN CREPT into the holding cell and shone onto the face of Titus, causing him to stir from his sleep. He was still groggy when he reached up to wipe his eyes, but the chains on his wrists that were secured to the wall kept him from doing so. He struggled for a moment, cursing under his breath, as he tried to shake himself awake after attempting to find just a few hours' sleep on a straw-covered floor. The straw was covered in animal dung and contained bugs that drew blood when they bit. He wondered how his brother had passed the night, for he could not yet see clearly across the cell. Titus could only see a silhouette of his brother Dumachus chained to the other wall, so he listened to his older brother's breathing to see if he was awake or still sleeping. He could always tell when his brother was asleep because he was a heavy sleeper and snored liked a wailing jackass. Titus smiled to himself at the thought.

Dumachus had always seemed capable of sleep, no matter the circumstances. Titus remembered when his brother had just robbed and killed a traveling family, including the children. He recalled arguing with his brother that day, and pleading for the children's lives, but to no avail. Dumachus had returned to camp and fallen into a deep sleep that night as if nothing had happened. Titus had often wished he could be more like his older brother, for the brutal acts of violence that he had witnessed over the years had always kept him from getting a peaceful night's sleep ... but this was his life, to be by his brother's side in an outlaw band of cutthroats and thieves, preying upon the caravans coming to and from Jerusalem.

Sounds from the hallway brought Titus out of his slumbering thoughts to become wide-awake and alert. He noticed that the sun had just crested the window and the cell was starting to become well lit. His brother was also waking up, for Titus heard him stir and softly began to curse. Sounds of heavy footsteps and muffled voices echoed down the stone hallway in front of their holding cell. Titus recognized one of the voices he heard as that of the jailer. The jailer was a large, foul-smelling man who seemed to enjoy his work far too much. At that moment, the jailer came around the corner escorting a large man who reeked of stale wine and was staggering and mumbling to himself. The jailer stopped in front of their cell and opened it. He escorted the man inside and placed him in a corner away from them.

As the jailer walked the man to the corner of their cell, Titus noticed this was truly a big man, one who stood at least two heads taller than the jailer—a very large man, but not fat like the jailer, either; Titus could see the man's muscles bulging through his wine-soaked tunic.

The jailer allowed the drunkard to plop down in the corner furthest from

the chained prisoners and then he turned
to Titus and sneered, "This drunk will
be your guest for a few hours, so do not
disturb him from his drunken slumber.
I have witnessed him crush a man's skull
with his bare hands, so if you two value
the rest of your worthless lives, keep your
voices down and do not provoke him." The
jailer smiled a gaping toothless smile, and
snorted a hideous chuckle as he left the cell
and locked it behind him.

By now, Dumachus was fully awake,
and in his usual foul mood. "The last day
of my miserable life and I have to spend it
not only in a cell, sitting in my own waste,
but now with the smell of stale wine and
vomit," he shouted. "If that stranger starts
to vomit, I swear I will break my chains and
go over there and strangle him."

"Settle down, my brother; stop trying to
scare a man who is too drunk to hear you.
We both have to endure the same smells
and conditions until it is our time to be
crucified," Titus said softly to his brother.

Dumachus simply smiled at his little
brother. "Yes, this is true, but *you* think

we should be in here suffering these harsh conditions for our crimes."

Titus sat still, allowing his older brother's words to seep into his mind. It was true; he knew deep inside himself, that they were finally getting their just reward for living lives as outlaws. "You knew as well as I, brother, that one day we would have to pay for thieving and murdering all of those innocent travelers, whether in this life or in the next."

Dumachus yelled back at him, "Would you rather I had let that soldier molest you when we were kids, instead of bashing his head in?" Dumachus' sly smile taunted his brother.

Titus remained silent, deep in his own thoughts and memories, for his brother had once again reminded him of how he had saved Titus from being raped by a Roman soldier in a bathhouse where they had been forced to work when they were just children. Dumachus had never allowed him to forget that day and to put it behind him. That day was the turning point of both their lives and had led them to this very day, waiting in a holding cell to be taken outside Jerusalem and crucified for their crimes against the State and the citizens of Rome.

In silence, he lay back on the cold cell wall and reflected on his life. What had truly led him to this day, awaiting death at the hands of the Romans? Was it simply an act of love that one brother had for another? Or was it something more? He realized the start of their downfall happened before they were even born ... many years before.

The lack of respect from the Jewish community had always inflamed his father, who truly loved his people, loved God Jehovah, and loved this land of Judea. However, this mattered not to the Scribes and Pharisees of the ruling class of the Jews. They considered his father and his family dead; none would speak to them, and that had made it difficult for their father to find any decent work. All of this because his father was born into a prominent Jewish family and his mother was a freed bondservant. His mother had been born into slavery when her mother's master, a Roman, took her against her will.

His mother had always said that she was an Assyrian and not of Roman blood.

The marriage of his mother and father meant that they had to live as outcasts in the slums of Jerusalem. His father nevertheless became a patriot and took up arms against Rome in a Jewish uprising. Both his father and mother had died in that battle; their father was mortally wounded and the Romans found him in their house being tended to by their mother—they were both killed in front of the boys' eyes. But the Jewish community did nothing to help him and his brother when they were orphaned and condemned to work at the Roman bathhouse in Jerusalem. Titus believed that this custom of being harsh and the lack of forgiveness of the Jewish community was the cause of their suffering since childhood. He did not know which were worse: the Romans or the ruling class Jews.

Just then, a rat ran across his legs and scurried out of the cell between the bars. Titus lost focus on his memories and looked up at his brother. "There goes our last meal, brother." Titus forced a thin smile.

JD SNYDER

He looked long into the face of his
brother, noticing the deep wrinkled lines
etched within his face, remembering that
had Dumachus not heard his cries and run in
to see what was happening that day, maybe
he would be more unforgiving and bitter
like his brother. He could never forget the
smell of the breath of the man, the sound
of the cracked skull, and the memory of
feeling the pressure of the man slither from
his body. Nor could he ever forget the sight
of his brother standing over the Roman
soldier with a large piece of wood in his
hand, the soldier lying with his head in a
pool of his own blood. To be subjected to
a life of crime at the age of twelve, simply
because his brother protected him from
being raped, had not been fair; they were
never given a chance to live a normal life.
Why shouldn't they have ended up here?

Titus had run similar thoughts through
his mind over the years of living as an
outlaw, but today it was different, for today
he was a condemned man reflecting on his
life. He had so often wished that he had
been born into a different family or that his

people had been compassionate toward him and his family... perhaps had even adopted them when they were orphaned.

Would life have been different for him today? Could he have grown up to be a merchant, an artist or even a scholar perhaps? He would never know, for all he has ever known was the life of a thief. All of these thoughts and regrets were in vain, for in just a few hours he would meet his death—not a quick death, an agonizing one that could take up to three days. He had witnessed crucifixion and he did not look forward to what lay ahead.

A smile broke across his face and he started to laugh gently, then louder. This apparently startled Dumachus; he scowled as if deeply puzzled.

"Have you lost your senses? Are you going mad?"

"I have not loss my wits, brother, but was just having the final thoughts of why we are truly in this cell awaiting our deaths. In all of these years of thieving, we have never been caught. It is because we followed Barabbas' crazy conspiracy to overthrow the

Romans that we now have to pay with our lives. If we had not chosen to take up arms against the Roman Empire and free Judea from its rule, we could still be living our lives. We have followed the same path as our father did over thirty years ago, and look where that got him! It's true that I hate being a thief; it is not much of a life, I will admit, but I would accept it over what is coming, brother. I am scared and, though I do believe that we should pay for our crimes one day, I think it should not be like this."

"Enough! Shut your mouth, you idiot," Dumachus growled. "The plot is still in play; do not destroy it all by letting our jailers know of it."

"Destroy what?" Titus now cried in a loud voice. "Barabbas is locked up somewhere below us in a dungeon, awaiting his own trial and judgment for his crimes, in which he will surely be found guilty and join us on a cross this very day. So, please tell me, dear brother, if our leader is in jail, and we are awaiting our own deaths, how can this plot still be going forward? You, I, and Barabbas are all dead men and our band of brothers will simply sneak out of Jerusalem and continue their outlaw ways under a new leader."

"Easy, Titus, control your fear. You were never very good with strategy—or killing, for that matter. We still have Judas in play, and our men are outside in this very garrison. We shall have an army of these Jesus followers rising up with our brothers and we will outnumber the Roman garrison twenty to one. We will succeed brother."

Dumachus said "When the word spreads that the Romans have imprisoned this Jesus on the eve of Passover, his thousands of followers will flock to the courtyard of this garrison and demand his release. Our men will be there, ready to inflame the situation and create violence. At that time, these Jesus followers will have no other option but to join in or be slaughtered by the Romans. Once the Romans draw their swords and begin the killing, no one in the courtyard will be safe."

"The key part of the plot has already been accomplished, for this man Jesus is in this very garrison, as we speak; Judas had done his job well and convinced the ruling Jews that he betrays Jesus for other reasons and has convinced them to demand his death. Since they already desire his death, it was probably not too hard a task. The followers of this new messiah will not allow it; they will rise up—just wait and see."

Titus reflected on his brother's words and on the plot that Barabbas had created months before. Most people in Judea, and especially around Jerusalem, knew of Barabbas as the leader of a large band of cutthroats and thieves. However, in truth, he was much more than this, especially recently. Barabbas had become a patriot and protector of the poor and homeless. He would steal from the rich caravans and give a portion to the poor and to those in need. He would also travel around the local drinking spots located throughout the slums of Jerusalem, buying free drinks for the poor and telling them how much better their lives would be, if the "Roman dogs could be chased out of Jerusalem."

At last, the people had started to listen and agree with him. Barabbas had been able to add hundreds of followers to his cause over this past season. Apart from the brothers, very few people knew that Barabbas himself was orphaned and made an outcaste at the hands of the Romans. Hatred of the Romans had created a bond between Dumachus and Barabbas for life, now it seemed, even until death.

Dumachus' body was starting to fall asleep, pinned to the cell walls. He struggled with his chains, trying to move around and get some circulation back into his lower body. Titus heard his brother cursing and slapping his body where a bug must have bit him. He ignored his brother's mutterings and continued in his own thoughts.

Barabbas had not only used hatred of the Romans to bond his band of brothers to his cause, but also many of the Jewish leaders. Barabbas knew that to be successful in an attack against the Roman garrison in Jerusalem, he would need most of the city's population behind him, as well as the Scribes and Pharisees—for they were the religious leaders and had great influence across the land. Judea had no army and Jerusalem had only some Jewish city guards, loyal to their Roman masters like the dogs that they were.

The problem had always been that the Jewish leaders, without a true king to rule them, could never agree on anything. All that the Jews would do was argue and debate in the synagogues. Without the blessings of their religious leaders, the people of Judea would never unite and take up arms again. His father had always said that this had been a problem for over a century since the Romans conquered Judea. This was why so many uprisings ended in failure; there was no unity.

Titus knew that these thoughts had kept Barabbas up many nights contemplating how to get his revenge, until one day, several months before, Barabbas had run into an old childhood friend—Judas Iscariot.

"Brother," Dumachus called out, "have you swallowed your tongue? You always have something to say, yet you have been sitting in silence. Do you not believe that the next part of the plan will be successful?"

Before Titus had a chance to reply, a voice from the corner of the cell said, "So, what exactly is this conspiracy and what does it have to do with Jesus? You have spoken a name that matters much to me."

CHAPTER TWO

TITUS AND DUMACHUS FLINCHED simultaneously, staring at each other and then slowly turning their stare toward the stranger. Earlier, Titus had noted that the big bearded man had greying blond hair when the jailer had brought him into their cell, and the cell was now lit enough to see that the stranger had blue eyes ... true signs that he was a foreigner. He also noticed that the man did not slur his words as most drunks do. Titus was astonished to hear the stranger speak to them in Hebrew, their native tongue. A moment of silence passed and the big man spoke once again.

"Did you not understand my question, friends? I am told that I have mastered your tongue since moving to your country. I pose no threat or danger to you; I simply need to know what this man Jesus has to do with your conspiracy. I am no longer a man of violence nor am I a Roman spy sent in here to listen to you. If truth be known, I have killed more men in my day than are probably in this garrison. I am not proud of this fact, mind you; it is simply the truth that I state. However, do me the kindness of not sharing this new information with our hosts. I do not think they would take it too kindly—and I am getting old and no longer desire to shed anyone's blood." The stranger smiled a broad smile.

Titus could sense his brother's anger starting to rise, but Dumachus controlled it and allowed it to come out slowly in the form of a question.

"Stranger, if you do not serve these Roman dogs, why do you pretend to be in a drunken sleep, all the while listening to me and my brother? We are nothing but two common criminals, condemned to be crucified in a couple of hours. What could you possibly gain from hearing the tale of two thieves?"

The stranger thought for a moment

before he replied. "On the surface of things, you speak the truth, for you are indeed a couple of common thieves that plague the lands—or at least that is what I thought when I bribed the jailer to place me in this holding cell with you. I traveled to Jerusalem in the early hours before dawn to do some trading at the market and to find the person named Jesus. When I learned that he was taken into custody last night, I presumed that he would eventually end up at this garrison; they hold the only cells in Jerusalem.

My plan was rushed; getting the jailer to stick me in this holding cell with you two, but it was the best I could come up with in such a short amount of time. Soaking myself in wine and acting drunk was a simple ruse to get the guards to allow the jailer to place me in here. I knew that I would have to endure these harsh conditions, but stumbling upon this conspiracy you speak of was rather surprising, even to a man such as myself. I thought I had seen everything this world has to offer."

Dumachus yelled at him, no longer able to control his temper. "You speak in riddles, you old fool; maybe you are drunk after all. There is no conspiracy; just two brothers condemned to die."

Titus finally spoke up. "Easy, my brother, it is you that are the fool ... to provoke this stranger who is the size of a small mountain, who could easily crush in our skulls, for he is not chained to the walls as we are." Dumachus' face turned dark red and veins started to protrude on his forehead as he sat in silence, listening to his brother admonish him for his temper.

Titus turned to the other occupant of the cell. "Please forgive my brother, stranger. Waiting for death in a bed of his own waste does not agree with him; please forgive his rudeness. My name is Titus and this is my brother Dumachus. Now, what is your name and why, if I may ask, do you seek this man Jesus?"

The stranger pondered his answer and replied, "Before I tell who I am and why I seek this man Jesus, I would like to ask you a question."

"Answered like a true Jew," Dumachus

blurted out, still seething at his brother.

"Ignore my brother," Titus said. "Hatred keeps my brother's bones warm from the chill of this cell. Please pose whatever question you wish."

"You argue and bicker like two old women. Are you two really brothers?" the stranger asked.

Titus gently replied, smiling thinly at the stranger's remark. "You pose a strange question, but I will answer you. We are brothers by blood, for we shared the same parents."

"But your name is Titus, which is clearly a Roman name and your brother is named Dumachus, which is clearly not Roman. If you two are brothers who share the same parents, how did this come to pass?"

"This man is either drunk or an idiot, maybe both. Do not play this fool's game; ignore him, Titus," Dumachus said in a loud voice.

Titus stared harshly at his brother, for he knew that Dumachus did not have any patience with other people, and then he turned back toward the man. "I was told that my father named me Titus, in hopes that my name would allow me to be accepted more in the world ruled by the Romans. Why he named *him* Dumachus, I do not know—maybe it means one born with a simple mind." Titus cracked a lively smile. "And since I have been by his side my whole life, I guess you can say we are indeed brothers by cause as well as by blood, for we have shared in all that we have done."

"Shared? We have shared nothing; you have lived on my handouts, little brother, since the time you were born," Dumachus said in a low voice filled with bitterness.

Titus' tone turned grave. "Just because I have never enjoyed killing and watching you and our band kill innocent people, does not mean that I have not earned my share of the spoils. It is true that I often wished life could have been different for me and I could have been allowed to choose another path, but you, my dear brother, would have followed this path no matter what options life had provided you, for you enjoy killing and thieving, like no other that I have seen. You scare me, brother, as you very well know. Some days, I would wake up in the mornings surprised that you did not slice my throat in the middle of the night to claim my part of the spoils after a raid."

Now Dumachus smiled broadly. "If it was not for the blood oath that we had to swear—that may have occurred, brother." His voice now had a slightly jovial tone.

Titus ignored his brother and turned his head once again toward the stranger. "Please ignore our banter; we have been like this since we were children. He has treated me more as his indentured slave than his little brother, so I am used to his barbs and his mean spirit. Watching your parents being killed and being forced to work as slaves can change a person's attitude toward life, for life can be quite cruel and unforgiving. We joined a clan of thieves, a sect known as the Brotherhood of Thieves when we were very young, orphaned, and on the run from the Romans. I guess you can say that they became our family.

"In the name of all that is holy, have you gone insane? Why are you telling this stranger our personal life story?"

"Because, brother, I am soon to die a horrible death and I want to have at least one person know that I was compelled to live my life as a thief, and I regret my deeds and all that I have done. Who else am I going to tell my story to? All you do is ridicule me for reading scrolls and trying to better myself. I did not choose this life, brother; this life chose me!" Titus stopped talking and looked down at the cell floor; he remembered that his death was only a few hours away and the pain and the suffering of being crucified was something that no one should have to endure. Silence filled the cell.

The stranger looked anxious. "Do not be concerned, I will answer your questions," he said hastily. He adjusted himself into a more comfortable position on the cold cell floor, listened for any approaching footsteps down the hallway, and frowned as if deciding how best to begin.

"I have had many names in my lifetime: one as a young free man living in my home country, one as a slave, one as a gladiator, another as a mercenary. The one I go by here in Judea is Simon. This name was given to me by my father-in-law about five summers ago when I married his daughter and converted to Judaism."

"I live with my wife, two adopted sons and my father-in-law at his farm, just outside of town. He has a large vineyard and raises sheep. I tend to the vineyard and bring wine to the market to sell. In Jerusalem, I am known to the wine merchants as Simon the Cyrenian, for I came from Africa, where I lived for several years hiring my sword out as a mercenary to anyone who could pay. There is much benefit to being known as a Cyrenian mercenary in the marketplace of Jerusalem; it keeps the merchants honest and the thieves at bay." Simon smiled a large smile and chuckled at his own jest.

This new information that Simon has just shared, brought both of the brothers out of their deep thoughts, for they had only heard of gladiators in the great arena in Rome. Titus watched a look of cunning cross his brother's face. It was obvious that Dumachus' devious mind had started to plot how they could use this knowledge and this man who was a trained gladiator and a mercenary to free them from their destiny. Dumachus quickly stopped being hostile toward this man; his voice became honeyed.

"Brother, tell our new friend Simon what he desires to hear; tell him what this man Jesus has to do with our conspiracy." Titus, with his mouth wide open, could not speak for a moment. He was thrown off guard, in shock that his brother would so easily agree to allow him to tell the story. Then he quickly reasoned that his brother wished to play this man, to use him in some way, and he wanted him to build some trust with this stranger, so he played along.

"You have intrigued my brother and me, for we are simple people who have never traveled outside the land of Judea. Before I share with you the information that you seek, tell us of your travels and life, for we would be most interested in your story; to hear your tale would be a most welcomed distraction from our present surroundings."

Simon looked puzzled, as if wondering how sincere they were about hearing his story. Then his words came flowing like a gushing river.

"I was born in a land that the Romans referred to as Gaul. Many clans lived throughout this land, never united by any king. The people would often fight each other, tribe against tribe, unless we had a common foe to battle against.

"Our land sat on the northern edge of the Roman Empire, so we had often united and fought Rome over the centuries. The Romans considered us uncivilized and pagan, and now that I have seen most of the civilized world, I have to agree with them. We were indeed pagans and uncivilized; but this was the way of my people. We would pray to the gods whose spirits lived in the trees; we were called druids."

"I have discovered in my lifetime that, whether it is the Greek gods, Roman gods, African gods, or druid gods, they are all man-made gods, with no truth in them. This is what brought me to your land, to seek out and find the one true God, the creator of heaven and earth. In truth, the last man that I ever killed was from this land of Judea. It was because of him that I came to live in your land."

"The last man you killed is the reason for you being in this cell? This makes no sense to me," Dumachus growled.

Titus leaned forward toward his brother to signal him to remain silent. "Be patient brother; let Simon tell his tale, as we asked him to do. Please continue."

Simon nodded and cleared his throat.

"The man was a scholar who had traveled to Africa to study some ancient scrolls that were discovered in a cave. He was a brilliant man; he could speak several languages and his knowledge of other religions was boundless. He was a Jew, but he did not practice as other Jews. I spent a lot of time with this man and had grown very fond of him. You see, I was given the contract to kill him, so I needed to get close to him to do so. He had many mercenaries of his own for his protection while he lived in Africa, studying ancient scrolls that were very valuable. I knew that I could not kill them all, so I hired out to him as his personal bodyguard. I would be by his side day and night for many months before I slit his throat. He taught me many things, for we would often talk after the day had finished. He was a brilliant scholar, a man of God, a man who I hope to see again in the afterlife." Titus felt a chill run down his spine when he heard Simon speak so causally about killing a man that he had both befriended and respected. This man may be worse than my brother, he thought; to befriend someone and spend time with him just to take his life was something that he did not even think Dumachus could do. Titus could sense the uneasiness in his brother.

Titus said in a soft voice, "Simon, this tale you tell speaks of what brought you to our lands, but why do you seek Jesus? Are you one of his followers? Do you seek to free him?"

Simon came out of his own deep memories for a moment. "I am sorry, my friends; this tale haunts my thoughts and my very soul. I have skirted the beginning."

"I was the only child of a chieftain of a small village and clan. One day, in my fifteenth summer, our village was raided by another clan. My father and mother were killed and I was taken prisoner, as was the custom of our tribes. The young men and women were often integrated into the clan who won the battle, sold as slaves or used in target practice.

"During that very same night that I was captured, I was able to free my bonds and kill a sentry while the others were celebrating their victory. I ran for three days and collapsed from exhaustion. When I awoke, I was a prisoner once again, but to another tribe's scouting party. They were on a mission for their chieftain and were to be gone from their village for many weeks. They had no time for a prisoner, so they sold me to a traveling caravan heading for Rome.

"In Rome, I was sold on the slave block in the slave market. During my travel to Rome, the master of the caravan treated me with kindness and allowed me much food and rest; I did not realize at the time that he was simply fattening up his cattle, before the sale to get a better price for his new young slave."

"Ah, so this is where your gladiator's days began," Titus remarked, nodding his head to his brother and attempting to straighten his back to ease the bite of the chains. He was now genuinely interested in Simon's story.

CHAPTER THREE

"I WAS BOUGHT, ALONG WITH SEVERAL other slaves, by a master of a gladiatorial school, the largest in Rome," Simon continued. "He bought me for one reason only—he got a better deal by buying the entire lot of slaves on offer. Later, I learned that this is always the best way of getting a good price. We were taken to the master's home. It sat above, but was connected to, the gladiator school and their training arena. My master had over two hundred gladiators and twice as many slaves." Dumachus pulled at his chains, trying to get comfortable while listening to Simon's tale. He tried spreading the straw with his feet, trying to ensure he would not be bit again by any uninvited visitors.

"I remember that we were all brought

into a holding cell, not so much different from the one we are in now." Simon stopped speaking for a moment as he gathered his thoughts. "We were stripped of our clothes and covered with a white powder to kill any lice. We were then escorted outside and placed onto benches where they shaved our heads. Afterward, we were lined up to receive our mark of slavery, a brand from a hot metal iron to mark that we were the property of his house. We were all washed by other slaves and then we were provided with tunics to wear. I remember this just like it was yesterday, even though it happened over thirty years ago; it was the first time in my life that I truly felt fear."

Simon raised the sleeve of his tunic to show the brothers a large scar where he had been branded. The brothers looked at each other, but neither chose to speak or to remark about the scar ... so Simon continued his tale.

"The next day, we were lined up in front of our master and his chief steward. We were looked over, asked questions, poked and prodded and then separated into groups. Some were placed into the house as servants for the master; some were sent into the school to serve as body servants to the gladiators, and others were sold to the gem mines or the mineral pits. I guess you could say that I was fortunate; because of my youth and my size, I was sent into the school to serve as a body servant for the gladiators. I was glad that there were other young men who were there with me, and that we slept and ate separately from the gladiators, for they were truly the most terrifying men that I had ever seen. I was taught how to be a body servant, mostly fetching water, food and wood. I later became a helper of the healer who was also a slave and lived in the school. I would help him make herbal ointments and herbal potions to heal the many cuts and wounds that the gladiators would suffer daily in training.

"By the time I had lived eighteen summers, I was as tall and as muscular as most of the gladiators, so my master asked me if I would like to train to become one. This was a great honor for me and I gladly accepted. Being a gladiator meant coin, women, wine, the roar of the crowd, and the love of the Romans, who all enthralled the games. It also meant the possibility of freedom, for any gladiator who goes undefeated for twenty matches in the Primus was given his freedom. Most do not ever get the chance to fight even one match in the Primus, the main event, much less win twenty matches, but it has been done by a few throughout history. So for me, there was always hope."

The noise outside the cell window was starting to drown Simon's words; he started to speak in a louder voice and more quickly.

"I was a gladiator for four years, fighting in the Primus only a half a dozen times, before my freedom came in another way. Rome loved their games and it was said that the arena could hold almost fifty thousand visitors. There was a section that was always held for the nobility. It had better shade from the hot sun and was high enough up to have a great view of the games. In the middle of this section was an area for the emperor himself, who would attend on special occasions." Simon stopped speaking for a moment, lost in his thoughts. "There is nothing like the roar of people calling out your name," he murmured.

"Speak up, for I cannot hear you," Titus called.

Simon smiled to himself. "It was not important, just old memories." He sighed loudly. "At my last match, there was a Roman senator who had just been posted as a governor of Cyprus, a province of the Roman Empire. He needed bodyguards and it was usual for the Roman elite to hire ex-soldiers or purchase gladiators, if they could afford to do so. Therefore, a deal was struck and I became the property of a Roman governor and spent the next ten years in Cyprus as his personal bodyguard. This was a good and pleasant time for me. The Greeks were noted for their love of knowledge and being in the governor's palace provided me with unlimited access to the best libraries and scrolls. You see, I had learned to read and speak several languages as a young body servant. There were gladiators from all over the world in my school, bringing with them their languages, religions and beliefs. Because I was young, and frightened of having my skull caved in or worse, I showed respect to all of them and learned from each of them all that I could. The ten years I spent in Cyprus were easy years, never having to kill anyone, being able to read, train and grow in knowledge, never without food or the warmth of a woman; it was a good time to be alive, even as a slave."

Sounds from the hallway echoed past their cell. Simon stopped speaking as footsteps approached their cell. He simply slumped down as if he was still sleeping, not prepared to continue his story until the sounds were well past. He silently watched as the jailer stopped by their cell and looked into it. He was carrying a large pail of water and they watched him as he descended the stairs to the lower cells. When no more sounds came from the hallway, Simon continued his story.

"But my easy life would not remain so, for one morning my master, the governor of Cyprus, was found dead in his bed. An investigation ruled that it was suicide and not murder, which was truly fortunate. If it was murder, I and his whole household of slaves would have been condemned to death. However, because he took his own life, in his will, all of his slaves were given their freedom. I had lived just over thirty-two summers when I became a free man. However, with freedom comes responsibility; I had to work and pay my way in this world. All I had ever been was a gladiator and a personal bodyguard of a disgraced governor—for it was later discovered that he was being indicted for bribery and theft and was to be taken back to Rome to answer to these accusations— so I did what came naturally to men like myself; I became a mercenary for hire."

Dumachus interrupted Simon and asked, "So how many men have you killed?" Titus gave his brother a stern look and turned back to Simon and nodded for him to continue.

"The path of a mercenary led me to many other lands and eventually to Africa, the Ivory Coast. There was always much work in that land, and the people and cultures were as diverse as the clouds. I dwelled in Africa for many years, hiring out my sword, until fate had once again looked my way and I took a contract and killed the man that I earlier spoke to you about. This is the man who changed the course of my life, and led me to this land of Judea. I came here to find your God Jehovah, and to find peace and solace. After dwelling here, I have found a beautiful wife, two stepchildren and a home. I am called a Jew, but I do not practice the religion. I thought by accepting this religion that I would find God and the inner peace that came with it. In truth, I have found neither, just a bunch of wailing old men who constantly complain of the Roman taxes that we all must pay and argue and debate over the words of their prophets.

"I had learned through my visits to the Jerusalem market about this man Jesus and his teachings. I was told that he healed the sick, restored sight to the blind, comforted the poor and even raised one from the dead. It has been said that he can forgive you for all of your sins and make you right with

God. I sought out this man Jesus to listen for myself what he had to say about God. I tried to find him in his travels with his followers, but to no avail. I heard rumors that he would be here in Jerusalem on this Passover. Upon arriving here, the word had already spread throughout the city that he had been arrested. Why he was arrested, that I do not know. I am to understand that the ruling Jews call him a rabble-rouser and a heretic, but the knowledge of what crimes he has committed against Rome escapes me. I cannot imagine a man who travels around healing people and speaking of peace to have committed any crimes. Now, I learn that he was brought here by betrayal and conspiracy."

Simon was startled and stopped his tale when Titus let out a low scream. He had just been bit by one of the larger bugs that inhabited the straw ... it must have drawn blood by the sound that Titus made. Simon heard Dumachus softly laugh in the opposite corner of the cell. He ignored the commotion and continued his story.

"The jailer, who you both saw bring me

into this cell, is, in truth, an old friend. We were mercenaries together until he received a blow to the head that scrambled his brains and left him in the state of mind that he now suffers. He is a harsh and violent man, but he remembers me well enough to accept a bribe from me to allow me to enter into this holding cell, so I may have a chance to see this man Jesus for myself, and possibly speak with him.

"I was told that most of the cells lay deeper within this garrison and the path to all cells must pass this one. My hope is that I may lay eyes on and speak to Jesus and ask him if it is true that a man's sins can be washed away in his heart, so I may finally find peace. So, to answer your questions: I am not here to free this man Jesus, I seek him in the hope that he will free me from the burdens that I carry within me.

"Now you know who I am and what brings me to this cell. I hope that you see that I speak the truth."

Only the many angry voices that carried into the cell from the outside courtyard could be heard for a while; for the brothers remained silent, allowing all that Simon had said to seep into their minds.

Titus reasoned that Simon was no longer the man he used to be. He was seeking peace. Titus looked at his brother, hoping that he also understood that his plot to use this man in some plan of escape was now futile, for this man could be of no use to them. He turned his head and look directly at Simon and said, "I do indeed, my friend, recognize the truth in the telling of your life and your purpose for being here. Thank you for sharing your story with us; we can see that you do not serve the Romans, but seek the man Jesus for personal reasons. I will tell you of the conspiracy involving Jesus that Barabbas had schemed."

Titus heard his brother yell, "You are crazy; you will tell him nothing. The guards may be listening."

"We made a pact with him, brother, and I do not intend to break it. No brother, I will honor my word, for it may be the very last time I get to show some honor in this life." Titus could see in his brother's face that he had resigned himself to allowing him to tell Simon the story.

"As I am sure you know, after each harvest, buyers and sellers would flock into Jerusalem. The buyers would mainly be exporters who would load up their caravans of camels and men and travel the camel roads that crossed all of Judea, bringing fresh-pressed olive oils, dates, wines, and scented oils for lamps to neighboring lands. This is why Barabbas would always be there in the market after harvest season, to size up those rich caravans and attempt to discover when and by which route they would travel.

"Barabbas would always make sure that many of our brothers were there at the market, selling their services as camel drivers or as caravan guards to the wealthiest merchants. This would ensure that we could always target the richest caravans traveling from Jerusalem. Once we were hired and on the camel roads away from everyone, we would slit a few throats, take the goods and sell them ourselves. We could live off the spoils of a few missing caravans for a couple of seasons. The camel roads are known to be dangerous and many caravans fail to turn up for various reasons.

As the story is told, Barabbas was wandering the Jerusalem market one day and came across Judas Iscariot ... an old childhood friend. It seems that the last time that they had met, Barabbas almost slit his throat, but only spared Judas because he recognized him just before he was about to take his life."

Titus watched Simon, as he adjusted himself on the cell floor to attempt to find some comfort. He saw a look of irritation sweep across Simon's face and heard him say, "I know all too well the Jerusalem market and the caravans that you speak of, for it is how my family makes a living. I have heard the many stories of caravans disappearing on the roads and of the bandits who plague them. Sorry to have interrupted your tale, but I have lost several acquaintances on these roads that you speak of. So your leader is not just a cold-blooded murdering thief, but someone who can show some compassion." Titus noted that Simon was no longer smiling as he spoke those words.

Titus felt a chill run down his spine, for

he could sense that this part of the tale has caused Simon to become angry—and this was not something he wanted. He continued with his tale, avoiding any more confessions about his deeds. "I was told that Judas had become a tax collector for the Roman Empire. Being a tax collector is considered a low job of no social standing, especially within the Jewish community. He would travel from village to village collecting the Roman tax that was assessed on every Jew in Judah after each year's census. Judas would travel with only a guard for the protection of the tax money and livestock that he would collect for the Empire. All Jews feared the Roman retaliation upon their village or city if anyone would harm a tax collector for the Roman Empire, so none dared to ever rob a tax collector ... no one that is, except Barabbas.

"As the story goes ... one day Barabbas and a few of his men were on the road traveling to their destination when they met and passed a Roman tax collector with his donkey loaded with a heavy burden and an armed guard. They allowed them to pass unchallenged, simply greeting the travelers as they would any others. As soon as Barabbas lost sight of them, he and his men ran for cover and started to track them. Knowing that they only had a couple of hours of daylight left and that there were no villages or cities within a day's walking distance, Barabbas knew that the tax collector would have to make camp. He would simply have to stay hidden, but close enough to see the glow of their campfire at night. After dark, Barabbas and his men would simply sneak in and kill the tax collector and his guard, then steal the donkey that was carrying the taxes that had been collected.

"Once darkness had fallen and Barabbas thought it was safe, they went into the camp and caught both the tax collector and his sentry off guard. They had both of them with blade points at their throats, ready to kill them, when one of Barabbas' men yelled out that the heavy burden was no longer on the donkey and that he could not find it in the dark. It was during the interrogation of the frightened tax collector about where he had buried the tax money that Barabbas had recognized the tax collector as his old childhood friend, Judas Iscariot. Barabbas spared the life of Judas and his guard that night and did not even steal the tax money that they were carrying. Instead, he broke bread with Judas and drank much wine that night and they told each other their stories of how they came to be a tax collector and a bandit."

As Titus was telling the story, he watched as Simon looked outside the cell to inspect the hallway, and then stood up and stretched his back and legs.

Simon said, "Forgive me; I know that you are in discomfort and cannot stand and stretch, but I am getting old and my bones ache sitting on the cold cell floor. Please do not let me interrupt. Your story interests me greatly."

Titus looked over at his brother and shrugged his shoulders, then turned his head back toward Simon as he sat back down. "As I was saying, they had reunited their friendship that night and Judas became a valuable source of information for Barabbas. Many seasons went by until they both met again at the market in Jerusalem, but Judas was now a changed man. He told Barabbas of a man called Jesus from Nazareth, and told how he had become a disciple of this teacher and how Jesus himself chose him to become his follower and student. Judas was tired of being a tax collector, tired of being despised by his own people. He told of how this man Jesus had many followers and more were flocking by the hundreds to hear him speak and witness him perform true miracles. You see, Judas believes that this man Jesus is the Messiah, sent by God to free our people."

Titus noticed that Simon had remained still as he told the tale of Barabbas and Judas, and how Jesus was connected to them. However, Simon looked confused or frustrated, and suddenly voiced what was bothering him. "As interesting as your story is, I do not yet understand how Jesus plays a part in your conspiracy. Time is running short, for the sun is starting to reach midday and you two are running out of time; speak clearly, so I may understand."

Titus now spoke bluntly, "I just

told you how Jesus fits into this. He has thousands of followers, all certain to be here in Jerusalem this very day for Passover. Add the hundreds of followers of Barabbas and we outnumber the Roman soldiers here in the garrison." He could see Simon deep in thought, as if he was still trying to fully understand. Simon said, "Maybe my mind has grown dull by the years, but what does a man of God who goes around helping and healing people have to do with any uprising against Rome?"

Titus looked over to Dumachus with a frustrated look on his face, and then looked back at Simon. "Since you did not grow up as a Jew, but only converted to Judaism a few years ago, you may not be aware of our history and the foretelling from our prophets. For me to make it very clear to you how Jesus fits into the conspiracy, I need to share with you some of the history of our people.

"Many of Jesus' followers believe that Jesus is the Messiah whose coming the prophets have foretold. Judas Iscariot believes this above all others, for he has witnessed his powers. I am sure that you have heard of the story of Moses and how he defeated a great Egyptian pharaoh, freed our people from slavery and eventually led our people to this land." Simon nodded his head to indicate that he had heard of this story."

"What you may not know is that this story started over four centuries before this event occurred. There was a man named Isaac who had a son named Joseph, who was the youngest of his twelve sons. Isaac loved Joseph above all of his sons.

"As Jews, our story begins with the betrayal of brother by brother, when Joseph was sold off as a slave to an Egyptian. As it was Joseph who had brought our people into the land of Egypt to save our people in a time of great famine, it was Moses who brought our people out of Egypt. They both accomplished these feats through the power of our God. Joseph used the blessings of God to interpret dreams to rise from a condemned slave to the most powerful man in Egypt, second only to the pharaoh himself. Moses used the power of God in the form of ten plagues on the people of Egypt to free those same people from slavery over four hundred years later. Both of these men are considered messiahs or saviors to our people."

"Since the time that our people were led out of the desert and into the Promised Land, with the Ark of the Covenant leading our army, we Jews have fought, died and bled to attain our inheritance. Most of us have continued to battle to keep our land from the many enemies that we have encountered for more than a thousand years now. During our times of occupations or threats to our ways of life, the prophets have always foretold of a Savior coming to help us in our time of need. From the strength of Samson to the courage of King David, our God has always heard our cries. And though he has indeed punished us for our sins against him, he has always sent someone to our rescue—a messiah!"

Titus stopped speaking as he heard his brother once again start to curse and kick at the straw-covered floor. He could see Dumachus pulling at his chains, trying to find a little comfort. Titus knew that his brother would not remain quiet for long, so he hurried his telling of the story.

"This is what the whole of Judea has been praying about for generations, for God to send another messiah, a savior to our people, to help free us from the bonds of the Roman Empire. I am told that this man Jesus is born from the house of David and is a Nazarene; so is the messiah that the prophets had foretold. This is why Judas believes that this man Jesus is the messiah that has been sent to our people to free us from our bondage, just as our God has done many times before. However, I am told that Judas has run out of patience, traveling with him for over three years now, watching him heal the sick, feed the hungry, and speak about some kingdom in heaven.

"Judas says that Jesus has not shown nor revealed anything of his real purpose or when he will use his powers to help free our people. So Barabbas and Judas devised a plot to force Jesus to use his powers and rally the people to arms. They believe that if they can get Jesus arrested and condemned to death ... this will cause him to use his powers, and inspire his followers to act.

Barabbas' men will stand ready to fight with Jesus and his followers at the right time. And this time is now—today!"

Titus could easily see that Simon was now starting to put the pieces together; he could see that he understood, for Simon was now staring at him as a young child would stare at a story-teller spinning a tale of great adventure…wrought with danger.

"My brother and I came to Jerusalem a couple of months ago to help prepare everything. Unfortunately, my brother got into a drunken fight and this brought us to the attention of the city guards. We were recognized as known associates of Barabbas and we were arrested and eventually sentenced to death by the local magistrate.

"Rome does not crucify common thieves and petty criminals, for if they did, the whole city would be lined with crosses. We are indeed thieves, but our crimes include murder and the killing of the Roman soldier who tried to molest me so long ago. It turns out that Rome has a long memory and our criminal deeds are well documented. We have spent the last two weeks in cells deep below, just being moved up to this holding cell a few days ago, awaiting word of the day that we would be crucified ... which is today. All we have heard so far is rumors from the guards and passing prisoners as to what has been happening.

"The last time we spoke to Judas, he was to go to the local synagogue here in Jerusalem and convince the head rabbis that he would betray Jesus and testify that he had been inciting a rebellion against Rome. The rabbis believed that this would be the only way to get Jesus condemned to death, for Rome cares not about the beliefs of the Jewish people and their religion. So Judas and the head rabbis were suppose to devise a way for Jesus to be arrested and convicted of inciting a rebellion. The head Jews consider Jesus a heretic and want him dead ... but under Roman law, a Jew cannot condemn another Jew to death, unless it is approved by the governor of Judea, Pontius Pilot. The only way to get Rome to condemn Jesus to death is to accuse him falsely of sedition.

"We know that Jesus is somewhere in this garrison, but so is Barabbas, for he was arrested several days ago. We do not know why or how Barabbas was arrested, but he had a bounty on his head and many people know him here in Jerusalem. So, this is our conspiracy, Simon—to create such outrage by the arrest of this man Jesus, that his followers will incite a riot and then our men can begin shedding Roman blood. Once the killing begins, the only end will be death, either for all of us or the Romans. I hope this now makes it perfectly clear to you how Jesus fits into our conspiracy."

As he was telling of this plot, the noise of the crowds outside in the courtyard was getting louder as it came through the window of the holding cell. Just when Titus saw Simon was about to speak up, the jailer appeared at their cell and beckoned Simon to come to him. Simon and the jailer stood close to each other for several minutes with only the bars of the cell separating them. The jailer was speaking to Simon in such a low voice that Titus could not hear their conversation. However, Titus did hear Simon instruct the jailer to unlock the cell. As the jailer was fiddling with the cell keys

THE TALE OF TWO THIEVES

to open the door, Simon turned toward
Titus and said, "The guards are coming
for you; they are minutes behind. We do
not have much time, so I will be brief. It
seems that your plan has worked partially.
Barabbas has been set free and Jesus has
been condemned to die on the cross ... next
to you two. From my many years in battle,
I believe I understand the hearts of men. I
am told that people followed Jesus because
he heals people and gives them hope. I do
not believe his followers will join in any
uprising, nor do I believe that he will do
anything but accept his own death. For him
to do anything else would contradict all
that he has done. I am afraid all you have
succeeded in doing is to help condemn an
innocent man to his death."

Titus was looking straight into Simon's
eyes when he said softly, "Die well, my
friend." He watched as Simon turned and
left the cell, watched helplessly as the
jailer locked the cell behind Simon and
followed him out of sight. Simon's words
were still echoing in his ears: ... *condemning
an innocent man to his death* as he watched

Simon disappear down the hallway. Titus' thoughts were interrupted by the sound of heavy footsteps coming toward their cell. He knew that they were the footsteps of the Roman guards, to lead him and his brother on their final journey, to their own crucifixion.

CHAPTER FOUR

S IMON WAS LED OUT OF A SOUTH EXIT, normally restricted to the guards and sentries. The jailer instructed Simon as to the path the prisoners would take to where they were to be crucified, a place known as Golgotha. Simon realized that this place was somewhere to the north of the garrison and he was let out a southern entrance. He knew he had a long way to travel and not much time to do so. He hastened his pace and started to pray under his breath, "Let me not be too late."

It took him almost an hour of weaving through streets and around buildings, before he came upon the path that he was seeking. Simon looked down the path toward the garrison and saw that many people had lined each side of the path, just a hundred meters below. He started his descent of the winding path until he came upon the mass of people. He stood in the back of the crowd and waited. Soon, the crowd started to cry out and yell and Simon looked up and saw the guards in formation heading up the path. He knew that the prisoners would be in the middle of the guards, so he started to work his way slowly toward the group. Simon knew that because he was tall and the street was narrow, he could easily see into the group.

As the Roman soldiers walked by, Simon could see that Dumachus was in the lead of the three, followed by his brother Titus, then Jesus himself. He could see that they were all tethered together by a long heavy rope; each heavily burdened in his slow passage up the pathway with a large wooden cross. He noted that their backs were so bowed from the weight that he could not easily see their faces. As he watched Titus pass slowly by, Simon knew that the next man must be Jesus. His heart quickened. He had felt this feeling many times just before battle. Simon's anger started to overtake his reason and he stepped forward toward the guards who were on either side of Jesus, as the battered man slipped and dropped to one knee; Simon's attempt to get closer was thwarted by the soldiers' shields and spears.

Simon turned pleading eyes to the centurion who was walking behind Jesus lashing him with a whip, as Jesus again slipped under the heavy burden of the cross he was carrying. This was the third time he had slipped and fallen within the last hundred meters. Surely, the soldier had the sense to realize further flogging would achieve nothing—Jesus was at the point of collapse. The soldier cast his eye up and down Simon's bulk, as the other guards were hesitantly telling him to stand back, and he seemed to have a flash of inspiration. The centurion smiled to himself, then pointed at Simon and shouted, "You! Come here and carry this man's cross."

The soldiers stepped aside and allowed Simon to pass. Simon now stepped up to Jesus and easily removed the cross that was pinning him down. He placed the heavy piece of wood to the side and he stood

I chose to carry My Sons crossed.

above the man he had been seeking. He only stood directly above him for a few seconds, but it seemed to be an hour. He was fixated on Jesus' back. He could see the bloody exposed flesh through his ripped bloodstained tunic where they had lashed him repeatedly. He saw that they had placed a thorn branch wreath onto his head like a crown. Then Simon was suddenly aware that the centurion had been shouting at him. "Get moving! Pick up the cross and get moving! We haven't got all day."

Simon ignored his command and bent down and gently gripped Jesus by the shoulders and helped him to his feet.

He was helping Jesus become steady on his feet when he felt the sting of the centurion's lash across his own back. Anger filled his heart; he released his grip on Jesus and was turning toward the centurion when he felt a slight touch on his arm. He quickly glanced back to find himself staring directly into the eyes of Jesus. Their eyes locked for only for a brief few seconds, but in those seconds, all of his rage seemed to vanish as quickly as it had appeared. Simon turned from Jesus, reached down and picked up the cross and followed him up the path to Calvary.

When they all reached what was known locally as the place of the skull, Simon noticed that there were already three holes dug deep into the earth. The guards cut the rope that joined the prisoners together, and then Simon watched Dumachus as he was led to the farthest hole, and Simon was told to drop his cross near the next hole, which happened to be in the middle of the two brothers. He wondered if the Romans had heard of Titus and Dumachus' constant bickering and simply wished to keep them apart or did placing Jesus in the center have any significance. Either way, Simon did not care about the reason; he was tired from the long climb with the heavy burden on his shoulder. He was no longer the young man that he used to be.

Simon laid the cross down, looked around at the crowd starting to form and he started to leave. He knew what was coming; he did not wish to see them in their pain and suffering. However, as he was slowly walking down the path, heading toward home, something stopped him. He was not sure why, but he felt it was important to stay and witness the deaths of these three men. He turned back and headed for the rear of the crowd now gathered.

Not desiring to look upon the men being nailed to the crosses and hearing their cries of pain, he kept well back of the crowd of people, looking instead toward the east. He noticed that it was midday, for the sun was high up in the sky. Such a beautiful day for such an ugly event, Simon thought to himself. He had always considered himself to be a good judge of the character of men. Whether he was born with this intuition or rather had obtained it as a gladiator, or over the years of serving as a bodyguard, he was not sure. The only thing that he was sure of was that, if he could look into a man's eyes, he could measure the depth of that man. However, when he had looked into the eyes of Jesus, it was he who felt that he was being measured; he could not shake the feeling.

He had also seen something in Jesus' eyes that he had not seen before. He could not find a word for what he saw in his eyes, but it seemed that Jesus only had to glance at a man to see his very soul. Simon did not understand the power that this man held, but he knew it was a thousand times greater than any intuition that he possessed.

Simon came out of his thoughts and notice that there were no sounds except for a few muffled cries coming from the crowd of onlookers. Thinking that all three men had been nailed to their crosses and placed into upright positions, he decided to turn around as he heard a loud, clear voice.

"Father, forgive them, for they do not know what they do."

He had just finished turning to see that the voice was that of Jesus. Why would he ask his father to forgive these people? Who was his father? This perplexed him … for he did not understand.

He started to approach closer to each of the men hanging, first to Dumachus, trying to see any expression on his face and to look into his eyes. Simon freely admitted to himself that he felt no compassion for he who was hanging to the left of Jesus. He had known too many men like Dumachus in his life, eaten up with hatred and bitterness, always trying to take their pain out on others. Simon knew that Dumachus took enjoyment in hurting and destroying others' lives simply because he hated his own. As he was approaching, he could hear Dumachus starting to curse and spit at the guards, his face displaying both anger and fear.

Simon thought to himself that maybe he was not so different from Dumachus after all; he himself might have had the same response to being crucified. He could see himself spitting at the guards and calling them names and their children names, in hopes for a quick death by the thrust of a spear. He realized that no man knew how he would respond to his own death, whether he would simply accept his fate or fight to the very end.

Simon walked around behind the men hanging, circling around to the other side to look upon the face of Titus. Simon felt a kindred spirit to this man. He knew that, like himself, Titus was placed into a life that he had not chosen, and had committed many sins against God and man. Simon contended that the only difference between Dumachus and his brother was that Titus felt remorse for his deeds and tried in his way to better himself. Simon knew that Dumachus saw this as a weakness in his younger brother. Simon however, saw this as a strength of character. Titus had a good heart, living in the midst of people whose goodness had left them long ago—if they ever had any to begin with.

Titus' face showed pain, but that was all; there were no signs of anger or even fear. Simon knew this look; it was a look of acceptance. He had seen this look in the eyes of several gladiators over the years when they had lain mortally wounded in the arena. They knew they were going to die and they simply accepted their death. For a gladiator, this was a good death.

When Simon turned his head to look upon the face of Jesus, they locked eyes once again, for Jesus was now staring at Simon. He watched as Jesus turned his face away from him and looked upon Titus. Simon followed his gaze and saw that Titus' eyes were now fixed on Jesus. No words were spoken by any of them until the guards came and started to push Simon away from the crosses.

Some of the guards had been below the crowd, filling their bellies with wine and rolling dice for the garments they had removed from the three prisoners. Simon could see that a couple of the soldiers were now filled with wine and were ready to cause trouble. He had noticed that someone had earlier placed a sign over the head of Jesus before they nailed him to the cross. The sign simply read: *This is the King of the Jews.* The guard, who had pushed him out of the way, came up to Jesus and started to taunt and ridicule him. Simon watched as some of the other guards joined in on the harassment; even some of the crowd started to join in on the laughter and ridicule.

It was then he heard one voice carry over the rest.

"If you are the Messiah, then free yourself and us."

Simon knew this voice; he instinctively turned to Dumachus. The guards and the crowd took what he had said as ridicule, attempting to join in the harassment of another hanged man to his side. However, Simon knew it was a desperate challenge … a plea, for Jesus to use his powers, if he truly was the Messiah. The harassment continued for some time, many people in the crowd of onlookers taking pleasure in their attempt to torment a dying man. Dumachus continued yelling at Jesus to free them and actually started to laugh along with the crowd; his pleas had turned to ridicule.

As Simon witnessed all these events, rage started to fill his mind once again, his blood flowing faster in his veins. "Let this man die in peace," he wanted to shout out at the top of his lungs. However, he did not need to, for Simon recognized another voice that topped the jeers and even overshadowed the voice of his own brother. Titus yelled with what seemed to be all his might, so his brother could hear him.

"Do you not even fear God, seeing that you are under the same condemnation? We are indeed getting our just reward for our deeds but this man has done nothing wrong. He is innocent!"

Titus lowered his voice, turned his eyes toward Jesus again and said, "Lord, when you go into your kingdom, please remember me." The guards, crowd and even Dumachus fell silent at these words.

Jesus turned his head toward Titus and said, "I say to you, today you shall be with me in paradise."

Simon felt a chill run down his spine when he heard the words that Jesus spoke to Titus. He looked at Titus and his heart filled with a sense of pride; tears started to well up in his eyes. He said under his breath, "A good death, my friend; you bring honor to yourself with a good death." He knew that Titus was not able to choose much of his way of life, but he was able to choose how he would meet death. He had chosen to have honor and courage with his last breaths. This was indeed a good death, Simon thought to himself.

He had witnessed enough; he looked at the sky and saw that it was well past midday. He turned and looked at the faces of the three condemned men for one last time and started down the hill toward his farm.

He hastened his pace toward his home, knowing that Sabbath would soon begin. As he was walking, he recalled the act of Titus defending Jesus and yelling at his brother to "leave him be." The sheer strength and energy it must have taken him to call out like that, while hanging nailed to a cross, to admonish his brother and defend Jesus, who he knew to be innocent of the charges against him. Simon wondered if Titus knew just how much honor and dignity he brought himself in the last hours of his life. For people like himself, who had been a gladiator and warrior, to die with honor and dignity was a good death ... for death was a fate that all men shared. However, it was the afterlife that Simon kept thinking about as he journeyed home. It was the last words he heard Jesus speak that kept ringing in his ears: "Today you shall be with me in paradise."

When Simon was just outside Jerusalem, something strange occurred that he had no explanation for ... darkness fell upon the land. One moment it was day, and then suddenly it turned to night. Simon turned toward where he had just left and he witnessed dark clouds accumulating where the three men hung crucified. He did not know the significance of this, only that he had never witnessed a storm and darkness cover the land with such speed and with no warning.

Simon felt confused by all that he had just witnessed, but he believed that Jesus was no ordinary man. If he truly was the Messiah, then the Jews killed the very person that God had sent to save them. He believed only one thing ... that no ordinary man would accept his death, ask forgiveness for those who crucified him and give hope to a criminal who was crucified by his side. He had witnessed too many deaths and he knew that Jesus was different from all others he had encountered. Simon knew that Titus was guilty of his crimes, and he was glad to see him accept his fate. However, Jesus was different, for he was an innocent man who had been conspired against and betrayed, someone who possessed something that perplexed him greatly. A sense of great sadness spread over him, for he realized that, years ago, he had started a journey for peace and forgiveness, yet all he had discovered were more questions and a more deeply troubled soul.

CHAPTER FIVE

I T HAS BEEN NEARLY FIVE YEARS SINCE that day in Jerusalem. Simon's father-in-law had passed away in his sleep about four years earlier and had left the farm and his estate to Simon and his family. Simon sat in the cool of a tree, stared out across his vineyards, and pondered his life. So much had happened in the past few years. He had never returned to Jerusalem since that day he had witnessed the three men crucified. God has blessed their labors, increasing their harvest and doubling their flock of sheep. He simply stayed on his farm and tended to the vineyards and his flocks. He found some contentment in tending to the farm and spending time with his adopted family. Besides, his own sons had become old enough to take the goods to the markets for sale and, since he knew the buyers at the markets, he believed that they would receive a fair price for their goods.

Sadly, his quest to find spiritual peace and forgiveness had eluded him all of these years. He hoped to find some redemption in the afterlife if the one true God would allow him to do so. Each time his sons returned from the market, Simon would sit down with them at supper and allow them to share any news they had heard in the marketplace.

Simon knew that the Jerusalem Market was always full of rumors and news from far off lands, as well as the current events of Jerusalem and Judea. A few nights before at supper, his eldest son shared some unusual news that perplexed Simon. For the past several years, his sons had reported the gossip about Jesus who was crucified and the astonishing claim that he had risen from the dead on the third day. It was said that he had visited with some of his disciples who had doubted his resurrection—and then disappeared, never to be seen again anywhere in all Judea. He was now called

Jesus the Christ (Christ being Greek for the Messiah, so Simon was told). Simon had also been told that Jesus had many followers—called Christians because they lived by his example and teaching—and they had multiplied in great numbers all over the land.

He would listen to this gossip about Jesus and his disciples. He learned that one of his disciples had hanged himself just days after Jesus was crucified—a disciple named Judas Iscariot, who, it was said, betrayed Jesus for thirty pieces of silver. He also heard that many of his disciples had fled the area, never to return. Simon did not know which stories to believe, for there were so many, with so many contradictions. On this occasion, his eldest son mentioned that he had heard that the leader of these Christians, a man named Peter, would be in Jerusalem this coming Passover. It was said that he was a fisherman from Galilee who was also named Simon, but Jesus had changed his name to Peter, and he was appointed as the leader of the other disciples and the followers of Jesus.

The news that Peter, the leader of these Christians, would be in Jerusalem the following week played upon Simon's mind. He had never mentioned to a living being what he had seen and had done nearly five years before. He simply listen to the stories and gossip without saying a word. Not even his own family knew of his story. Simon decided that it was time to go to Jerusalem and see this man Peter for himself. He wished to talk to him and learn what has been told and done in the name of Jesus and to learn more about his followers and his disciples. For the memory of Jesus had never left Simon's memories. He would often recall their eyes locking that dreadful day and the feelings that had overwhelmed him. Jesus had troubled his very soul for years now; it was time to put an end to it ... one way or the other.

At the break of dawn of Passover, Simon took a cart and donkey and slowly headed into Jerusalem. He was not sure what he was searching for or what he would say, even if he met this Peter. He knew that something had changed for him the day that Jesus gazed into his eyes. For that brief moment he felt a power of inner peace for the first time in his life and he wanted—no, he needed—to understand it. He knew it had something to do with Jesus, but what exactly he did not know. The time had come to discover the truth for himself.

Entering the Jerusalem marketplace brought many fond memories flooding into Simon's mind. He enjoyed the haggling, the stories being told and the sampling of the different foods and spices from all over the world. He visited his old vendors and greeted them warmly. They were all happy to see Simon the Cyrenian back at their tables. As soon as the word spread that Simon was back, crowds of people started to form around him, whispering to each other and pointing at him. Simon thought it strange that so many people would take such an interest in him when they never had before. He let it pass from his mind and asked one of his old merchant friends where he could find this disciple Peter.

The merchant told Simon where he could find Peter preaching to the people. "I am sure he will wish to meet you, Simon."

"Why would this man Peter wish to speak to me?" Simon asked.

"Because you are famous, Simon; you are part of the story of Jesus when they crucified him. Everyone knows that it was you who picked up his cross and carried it the rest of the way when he slipped and fell." All of the merchants listening to their conversation started nodding their heads in agreement.

Simon followed the directions he was given to where Peter would be preaching. When he had turned the last corner of the small narrow street, he could see a huge crowd around a man who was standing upon a rock, which elevated him above the rest. Simon found a resting spot in the shade far from the crowd, but close enough to hear Peter's words. He listened to Peter tell about the life that he had led for three years with Jesus, traveling around healing the sick, feeding the hungry, giving hope of salvation to the poor in spirit.

After an hour, the crowd began to thin and, when there were only a few remaining stragglers talking with Peter, Simon rose and started to slowly walk towards him. Simon noticed that Peter's eyes immediately fixed upon him, as he was walking directly toward him. Peter seemed to be listening to the person speaking to him, but his eyes remained fixed on him. Simon walked straight up to Peter and said, "Good day, Peter—they call me Simon the Cyrenian."

Peter took a step forward with a great smile upon his face and said, "And I am Simon the Fisherman, who is called Peter. My prayers have been answered, for I have wanted to meet you for a long time. I hope you are here to celebrate Passover, for I would like to invite you to spend this Passover with me and a few close friends." Simon had already told his family that he would be spending Passover this year in Jerusalem; he had the time and he needed to talk with this man, so he humbly accepted his offer.

CHAPTER SIX

BOUT AN HOUR BEFORE PASSOVER began, Simon started walking toward the house that Peter had pointed out to him. Upon his arrival, he was escorted to a large room upstairs, and there he found Peter and several other men sitting around a table talking. Peter sprang to his feet and approached him as he walked into the room. He felt a strong hug and a wet kiss on the cheek, as Peter welcomed him to join them. When they embraced, Simon noted that Peter himself was also a big man, tall and well-muscled … and not too much younger than himself.

"Please sit by me." Peter directed him to a chair next to his. Once Peter had made the introductions to everyone in the room, and the ceremonies of prayers for Passover were finished, he asked Simon, "Do you know this place where we spend this year's Passover?" Peter watched as Simon shook his head. "This is the last place where Jesus and all of his disciples had supper together; this is a holy place for us. In this very room Jesus revealed many things to us; his betrayal, his death and his resurrection upon the third day. None of us understood until much later what he was telling us. This room brings me both fond memories and shame," Peter said, lowering his head. He looked up again and said, "but before I share my story with you, I would like to ask you some questions, and you must tell me your tale of how you became the one the guards chose to help carry our Lord's cross onto Calvary that very blessed day."

"Blessed … there was nothing blessed about that day, I can assure you," Simon blurted out before thinking.

Peter simply smiled at Simon's remark and asked Simon to forgive him, and for him to share how he was chosen for the task. Simon looked around the table and noticed that all eyes were upon him.

"I was at the wrong place at the wrong time. Being a much larger man than most, I was picked out of the crowd when Jesus slipped and the guard thought he needed help to carry his cross. They simply picked the biggest man out of the crowd."

Peter stayed silent for several moments before responding. "Many witnesses tell a different tale. They say that you were moving forward toward Jesus and the guards were keeping you at bay, when Jesus slipped and his cross was crushing him. They say it was the commotion of you attempting to break through the guards to get to Jesus that caught the attention of the centurion who beckoned you to come forward to carry his cross. So you are telling us that all of these witnesses have it wrong?" Peter said to Simon with a light smile on his face. "I only asked because we are recounting the events that happened that day. Many stories and versions of what happened will be told and written for generations to come, and we would like to have an accurate account of everything that took place that day."

Simon's face began to turn red with

embarrassment; Peter knew more about the event than Simon thought he did. He replied once again to Peter, "A man called Simon the Cyrenian was chosen to help Jesus carry his cross to Cavalry: that is an accurate account of what occurred. As for the reason why and how I became chosen, it may not be wise to share this part of the story for all to hear."

Peter's eyes slightly brightened as he heard Simon's voice inflections upon the words "wise to share this part of the story." He nevertheless did not attempt to push the subject anymore, but became quiet and grave.

A scribe from the table looked up from writing something and said, "I agree with Simon; this is a story about our Lord Jesus Christ and what he suffered for all mankind. Having written that a man called Simon the Cyrenian was chosen to help Jesus carry his cross to Calvary, I believe it is an accurate account and that is all that should be written about this man. The account is not about him." All of the people sitting around the table nodded in agreement.

When Peter spoke again, it was as if he had tears in his throat, for the sound of sorrow radiated from his voice. "I have a confession to make to you, my brothers. I have told most of you before why our Lord placed a heavy burden upon my shoulders, to lead the other disciples and build a church in his name. I will share this part of the story again, so Simon may understand. One day Jesus asked us who we believed that he is. After several other disciples had answered, I told him that I believed that he was the Christ, the son of the living God. Because I answered in this way, Jesus changed my name from Simon to Peter and told me he was giving me the keys to the kingdom of heaven and that, on this rock, he would build his church."

"I was renamed for what I had revealed … that Jesus is the son of God … so all would know that I had spoken the truth. I was not worthy of such honor … for just several weeks later, in this very room, my Lord told me that I would deny him three times before the rooster crowed. No matter how much I denied this, it came true. For on that very night, I denied knowing Jesus on three different occasions. While my Lord was being tortured and crucified, I ran away ... trembling in fear.

"It was not until our Lord reappeared to us, after he was resurrected and told us of the prophesy that he had to fulfill, that I began to overcome my fear. Not until Jesus empowered us all with the Holy Spirit did we begin to understand all that had transpired. Very few people know of this." Peter fell silent and no sound could be heard from the whole room for what seemed an eternity.

Simon softly said," If only a few people know that you did this thing, why do you share this now with a stranger such as myself?"

Peter smiled. "Because Simon, this is a very special Passover." He asked Simon if he has noticed a few of his guest actually taking notes of what was being said. He went on to explain that these men were not only his trusted friends, but learned men and scholars. "I am just a simple fisherman from Galilee, and not able to read and write in any language except my own. These men travel with me and teach me new languages, as well as record events and stories for future generations. We need to have a written account of what has taken place as accurate as can be attained, so future generations will know the truth."

So! This was why Peter had invited me to Passover—so he might learn and record my story, Simon thought to himself.

He had indeed noticed men with parchments and ink, scribing words when Peter spoke. This is the main reason why he did not share all of the account of his story with Peter. Simon thought for a moment.

"So, you confess your shame for the entire world to read, so future generations can learn a lesson from this ... that one so close to his master, who was elevated to the highest among his disciples, was just a man, a simple fisherman from Galilee, who allowed fear to control his thoughts and actions for one night. That same man came back and today leads his disciples; doing his Master's bidding and building the church that his Lord commanded him to build."

Peter nodded in agreement.

"I, who have been a gladiator and

mercenary, know all too well this fear that overcame you that terrible night. For all who have courage possess it only by first tasting and experiencing fear. I would rather go into battle with someone who was overcome with fear and learned how to master it, than one who speaks bold of having courage, yet has never been put to the test. It is those who speak of courage, yet have never tasted fear, that crumble at the first sign of trouble and leaves you without support in battle." Simon saw a smile appear upon Peter's face as he spoke.

Then Peter said softly, "Thank you for your words of wisdom, my friend, for I was never a warrior, so I had never thought in such terms before. I made peace with my actions a few years ago, but forgiveness of oneself is the hardest forgiveness that there is."

"What do you mean, Peter?" It was one of the scholars sitting at the table who had asked this question. Simon sat quietly and listened to Peter's reply.

"We accept God's forgiveness for our sins through our faith in our Lord Jesus Christ. We then begin to forgive others who have trespassed against us in this life, as our master teaches us to do. But to forgive ourselves for our own transgressions against God and our fellow man... is the very hardest of them; though it is something that we all must embrace, if we are to truly gain the keys to the kingdom of heaven."

Simon heard himself say, "What are these keys to the kingdom of heaven?"

Peter turn to him and said, "When the Lord named me Peter he also told me that he was giving me the keys to the kingdom of heaven, as I have said, but I had no understanding to the meaning of this. These were not material keys that the Lord gave me, but more an insight into how to *unlock* what truly is of value, so we may *lock* and store these things that hold the greatest value to us ... for eternity, in the *kingdom of heaven.* It took me a few years of much prayer and supplication before I was able to understand this gift.

"I will explain this to you just as my master enjoyed explaining the truth to us. Our master often spoke in this way. He wanted us to truly discern what he was saying ... and when we could not, he would sometimes give us the answer to the parables, and at other times he would leave it up to us… He would simply say, 'Blessed are those who have eyes to see and ears to hear.'

"The keys to the kingdom of heaven are like a wealthy lord who gives a common poor man the *keys* to his palace. The Lord tells this man that the palace is his to do with what he will, for it now belongs to him. The man goes to his new great palace and finds that he has to use one of the keys to unlock the great iron gate that surrounds the palace. Once inside the courtyard, he has to use another one of the keys to unlock the very large, heavy front doors so he can gain access inside the building. Once inside the palace, he has to use another key to unlock another door that leads into a great study. As he proceeds into the study, he sees another door and unlocks this door and discovers a great library.

"In this great library there are empty shelves covering each wall, and there is a large pile of scrolls stacked in the center. The scrolls are so high that they almost reach the tall ceiling. The man believed that while there are many shelves in the library, there are not enough shelves to hold all of the scrolls that the pile contains. The man decides that he wants to place the scrolls that he wishes to preserve onto the shelves. He starts a fire in the fireplace in the study, lights an oil lamp and finds a comfortable chair to sit in while he reads each scroll and decides if he wishes to place it onto a shelf for safekeeping. He takes the remaining unwanted scrolls and throws them into the fire and watches them burn."

Peter stopped speaking and looked around the room while taking a drink of water from his cup. He was obviously trying to see who was truly paying attention; none but Simon's eyes were fixed upon him. A thin smile appeared on his face, as he remembered how many people did not understand his master when he had spoken in parables. He knew this was meant to be, for only the ones that the spirit chooses are allowed to understand truly what is being said. He continued:

"The man spends many years of his

life reading each scroll, deciding whether to save it or destroy it. Once he reads the last scroll and decides to place it on a shelf that is so full that he had to squeeze it into place, he stops and looks around the great library to see the fruits of his labor. The great shelves in the library are now filled to capacity with scrolls that he values most. Now he is prepared to enjoy the rest of his life within his new paradise. Through the many years of reading each scroll, the man had gathered much wisdom and insight to many things that were once unknown to him. He now understood why the great lord had given him the palace and all that it had contained. He opens the gates and doors of his new palace to the people of his local village, and shared all that had been gifted to him.

"Can any of you decipher this story that I have just told … as to what the keys to the kingdom of heaven truly are?" Peter watched as they all looked at each other in the room, whispering, trying to come up with an answer. He noticed that Simon simply sat still, seeming to try to place meaning on what he had just heard. When he saw nothing but faces wrought with confusion and bewilderment, he let out a small chuckle. "Do not be discouraged, my friends; I will share with you the meaning, for it is all part of why we are all here tonight. Please forgive me, but my master would often speak the same to us and he would watch our faces hold much of what I see on yours."

He smiled a loving smile at all in the room.

"The keys are like steps that each person must take to get to the next level of understanding. Each person must embrace each step in order to get to the next level ... or to unlock the next door ... as I described in my parable. Once you have truly reached the fourth level of this understanding ... as the man who reached the great library ... you will be able to start to choose what you wish to keep or possess ... in your paradise within the kingdom of heaven."

When Peter looked around the room once more, he still saw nothing but confusion on the faces of his most trusted friends. He thought for a moment and then said, "The Lord is allowing each of us to create our own paradise within the kingdom of heaven. People are as diverse and unique as the night's stars ... and so are our places in paradise. Our Master taught that the kingdom of heaven is like a house with many rooms. I have visited many houses and have stayed in many rooms in my travels over these past years. I know that every room is uniquely different ... as our places in paradise shall be."

"Whatever you wish to rid yourself of on earth shall be no more in heaven. Whatever you desired to possess on earth ... shall be yours to possess in heaven. I do not speak of material things, but of traits, habits, thoughts and ideas. For those who truly love the material things of this world shall have no place in God's kingdom."

Peter watched a look of concern cross a few faces. One scribe leaned back against the wall and folded his arms. Peter merely grinned and continued enthusiastically.

"Here are the Keys to the Kingdom of Heaven. Here is the Path to your own personal Paradise. The First Key is Redemption."

He held up a thick stumpy thumb and studied it. Eyes turned and gazed at his upturned hand.

"Come to the Lord with an open and remorseful heart, heavily burdened by your transgressions in this life. If you believe that Jesus is the Christ, the son of the living God and he died for all of your sins, and he has risen on the third day and reigns in heaven with God … you will receive God's forgiveness for all that you have done by sheer grace alone. For God loves all of us and wants to be reunited with each of us, so we may know our Creator and live in his abundance."

There was a rumble of assent. Suddenly it didn't seem too hard. One man picked up a tough loaf of bread and chewed thoughtfully on the end of it.

Peter held up a finger, along with the thumb. "The Second Key is Forgiveness." His voice rose to an excited shout on the word 'forgiveness'.

"To accept God's forgiveness, to forgive others that have trespassed against you and for you to forgive yourself for all that

God has forgiven you, is the only path to understanding. I have discovered that the last part of forgiveness is the hardest of the three. We all seem to have a desire to punish ourselves for our own trespasses when God has already forgiven us through grace." For the first time, Simon made a response. His face lit up as though he was looking at a beautiful landscape and he murmured, "Yes."

"As the law of Moses brought forth a covenant for the Jewish people and with it the ten commandments, Jesus has brought forth a new covenant for all people with just two commandments: To love God with all of your heart and to love your neighbor as yourself. How can we begin to love our neighbor, when we do not love ourselves enough to simply forgive our own actions, thoughts and deeds? We will all make mistakes and we will err in our judgments. Our Lord accepts us for who we are ... who we have been ... and who we will become. You must embrace self-forgiveness; only then, can you transcend to the next level."

Peter now turned as if he directed his words only to Simon. He sought his eyes and held them.

"The Third Key is Faith. Have faith that you are free of sin and are reunited with God ... and that he loves you unconditionally. Have faith that the Lord knows your heart and he will provide you with what you need on your journey through this life. He will see you through this life, and one day we shall all be reunited in the kingdom of heaven. For death is just the beginning of something new. Whatever obstacles are placed in your path, whatever tribulations you must endure, have faith that God will see you through.

The spirit of the Lord cannot flow freely through a heart that is clogged with shame. The mind cannot hear the spirit speaking when it is cluttered with doubt—be at peace. Have faith."

Peter opened his arms wide, sweeping them to embrace all the men in the room. There was an attentive silence.

"The Fourth Key is Trust." He raised one eyebrow, tugged at his beard and nodded slowly.

"You are now part of God's kingdom. … You must trust that you are free from sin and are now part of his family. Ask Him to enlighten you and show the path in this life that he wishes you to follow. Ask and you shall receive your purpose in this life … for we are all parts of the body of Christ. On your journey through this life, you may walk through dark and turbulent times … just know that you are not alone; our Lord is with you always. Trust in our Lord."

Peter put his cup down firmly on the table, and fixed his eyes upon Simon.

"For all who embrace these teachings shall be gifted with serenity and an enlightenment that will surpass all man's understanding … for it is part of your inheritance from our Lord. You will have many opportunities in your journey through this life to share what you have learned and what God has blessed you with. Share it with others, whenever an opportunity presents itself."

Peter stopped speaking and looked again around the room. He could see the scribes furiously writing, attempting to place these new insights onto scrolls for safekeeping. He could see some of his guests whispering in their own conversations, shaking their heads—and yet others starting to nod off after eating the Passover meal. He turned his focus once again upon Simon and saw that he was still staring at him ... staring deep into his eyes. Peter had noticed that Simon's eyes never left him while he was speaking, but he could not discern what he was thinking. Peter took up his cup again, drank from it and continued.

"While we were eating our last supper together in this very room, the Lord broke up some bread and handed it to each and told us to eat of this bread as it represents his body. He then raised his cup and told us all to drink from our cups ... for it represented his blood. None of us knew or understood the meaning of this, but we followed our master's teaching. We soon discovered that it was because he wanted us to remember that we would always be part of him ... the body of Christ." Peter then reached out and picked up a loaf of bread and shared the sacrament of the last supper with all in the room.

"We are all here celebrating Passover as our fathers have done before us, a tradition to honor a covenant that God made with our people many centuries ago. Abiding by traditions of any religion may bring honor to remembrance, but it will not restore any man's relationship with our Creator. Only grace can do this—and Jesus is the only path to this grace. While the traditions of celebration are important, know that religion was built by man ... to create a path for becoming righteous before God. Grace has now been given to us by God ... as the way for man to become right with him without sacrifices or sacraments. He had his only Son bear this burden, so all may freely be given this Grace. So remember to render unto man ... what belongs to man, and to render unto God what belongs to God.

"I have been given a mandate from our Lord to share these words with all nations on earth, so all may have a path to redemption and paradise. It is for these insights and truths that I have been named

Peter and chosen to lead this great endeavor ... to build his church where no floods or storms can ever wash it away ... for nothing on earth can destroy that which he has built in the heart of man. It is in our hearts where the Lord's church will exist. ... His spirit is ever guiding us. His church will withstand all things to come ... even the gates of hell and the sands of time shall not prevail against it. When two or more shall gather in his name, it is there, where his Church will be. As we are all part of the body of Christ, so too are we all part of his Church, which nothing can prevail against ... so long as just one believer walks this earth."

After Peter finished speaking, the room remained silent for several minutes. The scribes were still attempting to put Peter's words to parchment. Simon was now holding his head in his hands, thinking about all that was said. He thought to himself, Peter was given these insights by Jesus himself and now he had shared them with me. I finally understand why Jesus asked his Father to forgive those who conspired against and crucified Him, for they truly did not know what they were doing. And I now know why He turned to Titus that day and assured him that he would be with Him in paradise. Jesus was truly the Christ, the son of the living God, whose coming had been foretold long ago.

He now felt ashamed that he had hidden the truth of how he came to be chosen to carry the cross of Jesus that day, for Peter had freely given so much knowledge and had even shared in his own shame with him. Simon looked up and said to everyone at the table, "I wish to apologize for not sharing with you earlier the whole truth as to how I was chosen to carry your Lord's cross that day over five years ago. Peter, in his honesty and forthrightness, has shamed me into sharing my story with you."

Simon spent several hours telling Peter and the others about why he came to Jerusalem that day, hoping to see Jesus, of the conspiracy against him, about Judas Iscariot, Barabbas and the two brothers who were crucified with Jesus that day. Simon spoke about Titus and Dumachus, how they met, shared their life stories, and gave his view of how different the two brothers were in spirit. He spoke of what Titus said on the cross in defense of Jesus against his own brother and what Jesus had said to Titus when he asked to be remembered in his kingdom.

Simon noticed that Peter's eyes began to moisten and tears were running down his cheeks when he was telling his story. "I did not mean to offend you, Peter," he said.

Peter wiped his tears and said, "You did not offend me, my friend; you simply answered so many unanswered questions."

"My tears are for my Lord, for He knew of this conspiracy against Him and He spoke of this to us in this very room. None of us understood then what He was speaking about. He knew how He was going to be betrayed and that He would be crucified. He knew that this was God's will and He had to obey the will of his Father. It has been written that one man brought us into sin and one man must bring us out, so we may be forever reunited with our Creator."

"My tears are also for Judas. You see, he was like a brother to me and I know that he loved our Master as much as I did. I never believed that he would betray our Lord for money alone. And when he was found hanged, I thought it strange to hear that there were thirty pieces of silver lying at his feet. I think he was trying to leave a message, that he did not betray the one he loved for money. You have explained that he betrayed our Master in the hope that he would use his power to free our people. I am inclined to believe this, for it makes more sense to me than for him to betray the one he so loved for a few coins. My heart breaks for Judas, for he sacrificed his place in the kingdom because he simply did not understand how Jesus was going to free our people—not just our people, but every person on earth who would simply believe."

Peter recomposed himself and said in a stern voice, "Our Lord warned us that there would be people committing evil believing that they are doing acts of good. Let the acts of Judas live on as a testimony of how one man can do such evil, thinking that he was doing good.

Simon felt a sense of relief flow through

his body and was glad to hear that he had not offended Peter. He could see the sorrow in Peter's eyes when he spoke of Jesus, and he could tell that he had truly loved Judas as a brother. As Simon dwelt upon all that has been said, he could feel tears start to well in his eyes. This troubled him, for the last time he felt this sensation was the day that he watched the three men being crucified. This sensation was foreign to him for he had not actually shed tears since he was a small boy. He tried to clear his mind and focus on Peter, as the apostle began to speak to him directly.

"As far as your tale of the two brothers, this is quite a story. We have already written down the account of what Jesus said to the criminal who was hung to his right, for this is a great lesson to be learned by all. It is never too late to ask for redemption, as long as you have breath in your lungs and life in your body. Since our Lord's resurrection, this story has already spread across the lands. We did not know the names of the two who were crucified with Jesus, just that they were condemned as criminals and thieves to be crucified. For me, this explains why the thief to the right of Jesus would speak up and defend him against the thief on the Lord's left. The knowledge that they were brothers and they argued constantly makes sense of these events for me."

Peter clasped Simon's shoulder.

"I can see by the way you speak of the two brothers, that you held Titus with some regard," he continued. "Your friend Titus was a brave man; he defended Jesus against his own brother while hanging on the cross, and it shames me, because, as you know, I was in hiding, denying that I knew him." He looked up to the ceiling for a moment and said, "Truly blessed are those, Lord, who by simply hearing the word, believe in you."

Peter picked up a pitcher of water and stood up next to Simon who was still seated. "I wish to give you a gift—the same gift my Lord Jesus gave me, if you will accept." Simon bowed his head, and then Peter poured some water on the top of his head, laid his hands on his head, and began to pray.

CHAPTER SEVEN

A FEW YEARS LATER, SIMON WAS back at his farm working in the vineyard, attempting to remember a verse of a poem that he had recently heard someone recite. His memory was not what it once was, for age was catching up on him. He thought that the verse went something like "Some say he was just a prophet, some say he was just a man—but the dumb and blind will always try to guess the best they can. He sacrificed his life the day that they nailed him to the cross, but he died not for the righteous, but for the sinners and the lost." Simon could not remember the rest of the verse; he told himself that he needed to start to write things down that he wanted to remember for more than a couple of days.

He was simply glad that he was able to share his story with his family that same day he had returned home from Jerusalem years ago. His two adopted sons and his wife allowed him to baptize them and welcome them into his Master's kingdom. Simon had been searching for the one true God for many years, and finally had found him through his Lord and Savior, Jesus Christ. He had embraced Peter's teachings that day and had discovered the inner peace and serenity that he had been searching for. The burden of all the sins that he carried for years had finally been lifted from him. He had been made whole, a complete person who could truly enjoy the rest of his days on earth.

Attempting to remember the poem caused Simon to reflect back to that day that he looked into the eyes of Jesus and felt the power that resonated from him. He also thought about Titus and was saddened that no one would ever know the truth about all that happened that day. The name of his friend Titus would be forever lost, the whole conspiracy against Jesus never told, and his own story of what occurred never revealed ... for the scribes decided not to record all of what Simon and Peter had shared that day when he accepted Jesus as his Lord. Simon would never forget ... for it was the courage and faith that Titus displayed that day that had sown the seed of change into his heart and prepared him to accept Jesus as his Lord and savior that night Peter had offered to baptize him; all of the insight and wisdom that Peter had shared that night had opened his eyes to the truth.

Simon thought about all of the lives that had intertwined that day, and knew in his heart that it was not merely coincidence. It was part of God's plan for him. He recalled a verse that someone had once shared with him: *Seek the truth and the truth shall set you free.* ... He wondered if the person who had shared it with him truly understood its meaning.

Simon and his wife had decided to honor her family's ancestors and continue to follow her family's traditions. He did not mind honoring the remembrance of God's first covenant with his people. This brought comfort and honor to his wife and adopted sons. It also brought peace and tranquility living amongst his Jewish neighbors. He remembered what Peter had told him about rendering unto man what belongs to man, and to God what belongs to God. Simon would wake each morning before the sun had crested the hill that sat east of their farm. He would pray and rejoice each day, that he would never have to be burdened with sin again, or face the challenges in life alone, for Jesus lives on in his heart. He knew the truth of the afterlife and what paradise would be like for him and his family, for they would be together in heaven. Such peace and contentment that the Lord had given him could not be put into words, but he wished that he could, for he believed that the Lord wanted everyone to share in this gift that he had been given. Just then, it struck him; an idea raced through his mind as fast as a lightning bolt through the night sky. He dropped what he was doing and started briskly towards his house.

Sitting at his ivory colored desk, where he would spend hours doing the tally for his goods to be taken to the market, he decided to do something different this day. Although his memory was indeed starting to fade, his memory of what occurred the day his Lord and Savior had been crucified was as fresh in his mind as if it had happened yesterday. He recalled what Peter had told him about how the Lord would place a path for him to follow. He smiled to himself and shook his head in disbelief that it had taken him so long to understand his purpose and what the Lord wanted him to do. He took out a piece of parchment from his desk and unrolled it. He bowed his head and prayed: "Lord, your will be done."

Simon smiled, picked up a quill and started to write his story—*The Tale of Two Thieves.*

INFORMATION

For a personalized signed copy, go to:
www.taleoftwothieves.com

To email me personally, please do so at:
jdsnyder@taleoftwothieves.com

For Correspondence - Write Me @
JD Snyder
4888 N Kings Hwy #217
Fort Pierce, Fl 34951

Please...Tell your friends!